LEMONADE SUN

And Other Summer Poems

WordSong
An Imprint of Highlights
815 Church Street
Honesdale, Pennsylvania 18431
wordsongpoetry.com
Printed in China

Library of Congress Cataloging-in-Publication Data
Dotlich, Rebecca Kai.
Lemonade sun: and other summer poems / by Rebecca Kai Dotlich ;
illustrated by Jan Spivey Gilchrist.—1st ed.
[32]p. : col. ill. ; cm.
Summary : A collection of poems celebrating summer sights and sounds.
ISBN: 978-1-56397-660-5 (hc) • ISBN: 978-1-56397-944-6 (pb)
1. Summer—Children's poetry. [1. Summer—poetry.] I. Gilchrist, Jan Spivey, ill. II. Title.
811.54—dc21   1998   AC   CIP
97-74192

First edition
First Boyds Mills Press paperback edition, 2001
Book designed by Tim Gillner
The text of this book is set in Souvenir.
The illustrations are done in acrylic.

15 14 13 12 11

LEMONADE SUN

And Other Summer Poems

By Rebecca Kai Dotlich

Illustrated by Jan Spivey Gilchrist

WORDSONG

AN IMPRINT OF HIGHLIGHTS

Honesdale, Pennsylvania

Contents

LEMONADE SUN

Popsicle stains.
Fudgesicle fun.
Strawberry sizzle—
lemonade sun.

A CIRCLE OF SUN

I'm dancing.
I'm leaping.
I'm skipping about.
I gallop.
I grin.
I giggle.
I shout.
I'm Earth's many colors.
I'm morning and night.
I'm honey on toast.
I'm funny.
I'm bright.
I'm swinging.
I'm singing.
I wiggle.
I run.
I'm a piece of the sky
in a circle of sun.

LEMONADE

We pour
its liquid sweetness
from a tall
glass pitcher,
splashing
sunshine
on frosty squares
of ice,
lemon light
and slightly tart,
we gulp its gold—
licking our lips
with summer.

MY LEMONADE STAND

**Cookies for sale!
And cake! One dime!**
That's what it says
on my cardboard sign.
I pile cookies on a plate.
I eat just one
and then, I wait . . .
I taste the cake
(one tiny slice)
I squeeze the lemons
and stir the ice;
I count and stack
the paper cups . . .
**fresh lemonade
is coming up!**
I count the bruises
on my knee . . .
won't somebody buy something,
please?

9

SUNFLOWERS

Yellow faces
round
as plates;
giants growing
at the gate.
Golden guards
saluting
sky;
garden kings
with chocolate eyes.

SUMMER GREETINGS

Today's the day
that summer comes.
Good-bye to cold;
hello to sun!
Hello to rose
and vines of green,
to lettuce leaves—
oh, hello beans!
Today's the day
for climbing trees,
for jumping rope
and skinning knees,
for swinging high
and skipping fast,
and reading
books
outside
at last.

BACKYARD BUBBLES

One bubble
shimmies
from the wand
to waltz around
the backyard lawn.
One fragile globe
of soapy skin—
a glimmering
of breath within
a perfect pearl,
I blow again!
One more bubble
squeezes through,
one blushing bead
of water-blue;
and then
another
rinsed in pink
(shivering
with pastel ink)
dances on
a summer sigh,
shimmering
with shades of sky,
s-l-o-w-l-y slides
right out of sight;
backyard bubbles
taking flight.

DRAGONFLY

This sky-ballerina,
this glimmering
jewel,
glides in a gown
of lucid blue—
with wings that you
could *whisper* through.

BUMBLEBEES

Bees have teeny,
tiny eyes,
and teensy-
weensy wings.
Bees have itty-
bitty legs,
but JUMBO,
GIANT
stings.

MARBLES

Rolling
clicking,
rolling,
clacking,
tiger-eyes
and glass moons
crashing;
rainbows spinning
on and on—
pocket treasures,
sidewalk songs.

LADYBUG

Smaller
than a button,
bigger than a spot
this crimson queen
with midnight polished
polka dots
journeys in
her ruby shell,
across
the walks,
along
the cracks,
among
the petals of a rose—
carefully,
tenderly she goes.

DANDELION DAYS

Lemon lions;
dandy
lions,
dance beside
the clover;
wearing hats
of whisper-white
when summer days
are over.

DOUBLE DUTCH SONG

Climb the mountain,
cross the sea.
Who do I love?
Who loves me?
Over, under,
pick a name;
Johnny, Jacob,
Joseph, James . . .
climb the mountain,
cross the sea.
How many wishes
can there be?
One, two, three, four—
over, under,
out the door!

THE GIANT SEEKER

Riding high
on daddy's shoulders,
bouncing in
and out of wind,
I reach for giants.
Playing hide-and-seek
with soft-skinned leaves
of summer,
we glide
across the lawn;
Daddy
prances on,
galloping
from tree to tree,
watch your head!
he sings;
I am the giant seeker
on the back
of a king.

18

BALLOON SEND OFF

Tap-tap-tapping
the soft-bellied drum
along my knuckles
and my thumb,
when suddenly
its squeaky skin
goes skipping off
into the wind;
waltzing on
the summer air—
and just to think
I put it there!

BUTTERFLY

I like the easy
way you go,
floating
freely,
flying
low,
and, oh!
to be
a butterfly,
sailing on
one *breath* of sky.

BAREFOOT

Feet
bare as babies,
touching
the tickle
of new grass,
wearing
dandelions
between warm toes,
dressed
in wild jewels
of summer.

SIDEWALK SONGS

Up and down
and all day long,
we sing summer
sidewalk songs;
Dreamsicles cold,
Dreamsicles sweet,
skipping out a barefoot beat—
brown as ginger,
warm as toast,
we love sidewalk
songs the most.

WILDFLOWERS

Lavender blue.
Willful,
wild.
A summer meadow's
mountain child.
Giggling pink,
tumbling
gold;
never doing
what they're told!

PINWHEELS

Round
and round
and round they go;
carnival colors
whirl
and blow;
faster, faster!
Swirl and spin;
on wooden sticks
they rainbow-ride
the wind.

JACKS

Tossed
quickly
from an eager fist,
this silver-mix
goes somersaulting,
silver
falling to the walk,
raining
tin bouquets;
small bundles
of piggyback
stars.

JELLYFISH

Who would have thought
blobs we see through,
could be so cruel
yet *crystal-blue*?

JUMP ROPE RHYME

Skip, skip!
Fast and slow,
all the way to Idaho.
Skip to Texas.
Skip to Maine—
skipping all the way
to Spain.
Jump, jump!
Up and down,
all the way to
Chinatown.
Skip to Denmark.
Skip to Rome—
around the world,
then go back home!

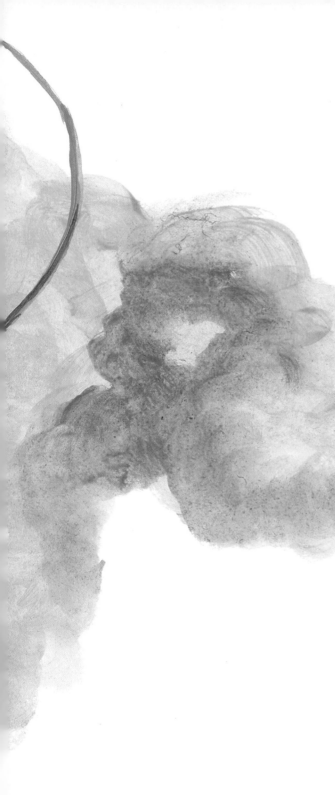

JUMP ROPE TALK

Jumping, jumping,
Double Dutch
on cement sidewalks
cooled by dusk.
Down in the meadow
where the green grass grows,
there sits Sophie sniffin' at a rose—
Our voices echo
in the air,
Turn around, turn around,
teddy bear—
The street and porch
lights stagger on;
we jump, jump, jump,
and chant these songs:
Peppers are red
and berries are blue,
pick a name to follow you—
Our voices ring
beneath the stars,
Skip to Venus,
jump to Mars—
Jumping, jumping,
Double Dutch,
Mama's got her silver
in the hutch—
we're singing songs
on cracked sidewalks,
Papa keeps his money
in his sock—
to the slap, slap, slap
of jump rope talk!

SUMMER SWINGING

Up and away
to the moon and down,
up to the brightest stars.
My feet reach up,
my feet fall back;
I'm climbing up to Mars.
I bend my knees,
then s-t-r-e-t-c-h my legs,
as back-and-forth I fly,
my barefoot toes
touch every star
that's shining in the sky.
Over the hills
and over the earth,
I swing,
I sing,
I shout.
I close my eyes,
I hold my breath,
and I . . .
jump out!

STARS

One hundred and eight,
one hundred and nine—
I'm counting the stars
one
at a time;
like splinters
of diamonds,
like slivers
of pearls,
like sequins of light
they *sparkle*
the world.

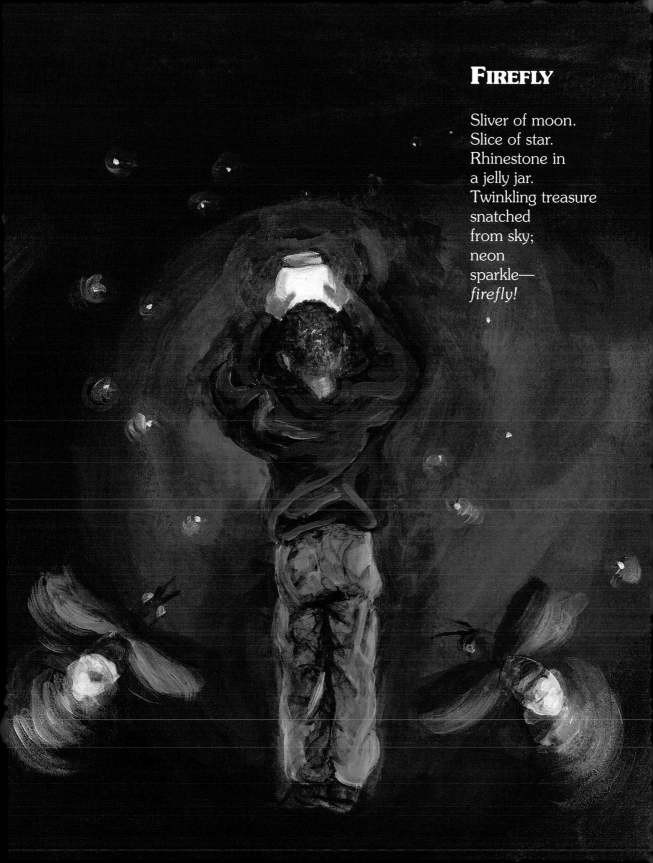

FIREFLY

Sliver of moon.
Slice of star.
Rhinestone in
a jelly jar.
Twinkling treasure
snatched
from sky;
neon
sparkle—
firefly!

FIREWORKS

Emerald glitter
fills the sky;
a thousand dashing
dragon eyes
sparkle! flash!
spiral,
climb—
leaping,
leaving Earth
behind.
Roman candles
sizzle,
shatter,
diamonds dazzle,
rubies
scatter,
spilling silver
stars of fire—
blasting bits
of copper wire.
Sapphires crumble
in the sky,
tinsel
tumbles
down to die,
onto city streets
and roads;
CRACKLE—
POP!
The sky
explodes!

STAR WISH

Instead of always
being far
up in the sky
I wish a star
would fall into
my own backyard;
a glowing chip,
a silver shard
of galaxy
so I could say—
I held a piece of star
today!

NIGHTDANCE

All over the world
there are nightdance children;
hiding,
hopping,
never stopping—
jump rope rhyming,
late hopscotching—
happy feet
in chalky squares;
children dancing
everywhere.
And the sun comes up,
and the sun goes down,
and children moon-skip
all around,
as fireflies flicker
in the air—
There are nightdance children
everywhere.